Dear Parent:

Your child's love of reading starts here!

Every child learns to read in a different way and at his or her own speed. Some go back and forth between reading levels and read favorite books again and again. Others read through each level in order. You can help your young reader improve and become more confident by encouraging his or her own interests and abilities. From books your child reads with you to the first books he or she reads alone, there are I Can Read Books for every stage of reading:

SHARED READING
Basic language, word repetition, and whimsical illustrations, ideal for sharing with your emergent reader

BEGINNING READING
Short sentences, familiar words, and simple concepts for children eager to read on their own

READING WITH HELP
Engaging stories, longer sentences, and language play for developing readers

READING ALONE
Complex plots, challenging vocabulary, and high-interest topics for the independent reader

I Can Read Books have introduced children to the joy of reading since 1957. Featuring award-winning authors and illustrators and a fabulous cast of beloved characters, I Can Read Books set the standard for beginning readers.

A lifetime of discovery begins with the magical words "I Can Read!"

Visit www.icanread.com for information
on enriching your child's reading experience.

Baby Shark and the Magic Wand

© Smart Study Co., Ltd. All Rights Reserved.

Pinkfong™ and Baby Shark™ are trademarks of Smart Study Co., Ltd.,

registered or pending rights worldwide. © 2021 Viacom International Inc.

All Rights Reserved. Nickelodeon is a trademark of Viacom International Inc.

Printed in the United States of America.

ISBN 978-0-06-296590-5

21 22 23 CWM 10 9 8 7 6 5 4 3

❖

First Edition

pinkfong
BABY SHARK™

Baby Shark
and the
Magic Wand

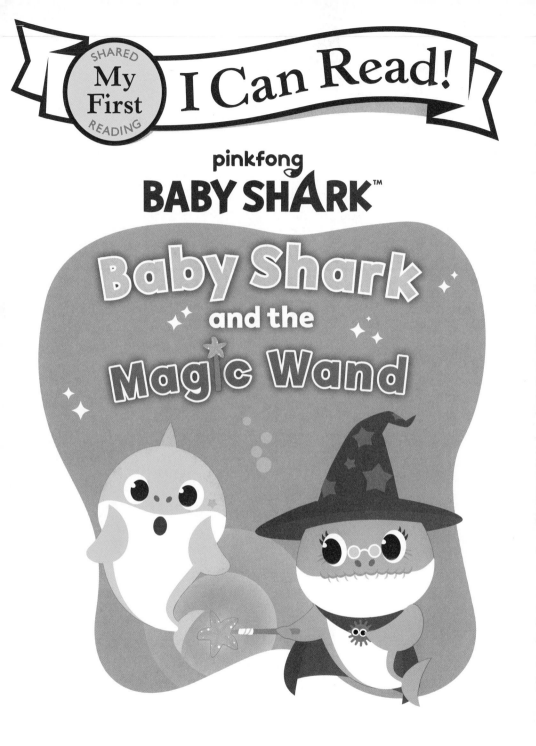

HARPER
An Imprint of HarperCollinsPublishers

Baby Shark Family & Friends

Baby Shark

Mommy Shark

Daddy Shark

Magic Wand

Grandma Shark

Grandpa Shark

Grandma Shark has
a magic wand.
"Poof!" she says.
"My wand can do anything!"

Grandma Shark sees a
baby fish.
"Boo-hoo," he says.
"Please find my mommy."

"Poof!" Grandma Shark says.

The fish's mommy comes back!

Grandma Shark sees
a pink fish.
"I need a house!"
the pink fish says.

"Poof!" Grandma Shark says.

The fish gets a new house!

"Thanks!" the baby fish says.

"You found my mommy!"

"Yay!" the pink fish says.

"I love my house."

Grandma Shark is so happy,
she twirls her wand.
But it falls and breaks!

Grandma Shark fixes her wand.
Then Baby Shark asks,
"Can you turn my ball
into a friend?"

"Hmm," Grandma Shark says.
"I hope this works . . . poof!"

"Oh no!" Grandma Shark says.

The broken wand
turned Baby Shark into a toy!
Grandma Shark has to fix it!

The wand sparkles.

"Phew!" Grandma Shark says.
"That worked!"
Baby Shark is back to normal.

Then Grandma Shark
sees Mommy Shark.
"Can you make
my pencil longer?"
Mommy asks.

"Hmm," Grandma Shark says.
"I hope this works . . . poof!"

"Oh no!" Mommy Shark says.
"It got even shorter."

"I'll try again," Grandma says.
"Poof!
That worked!"

"Grandma Shark!"
Baby Shark says.
"Can you help me
build my sand castle?"

Grandma Shark does
anything for Baby Shark.
"Of course!" she says.

"Now," Grandma Shark says.
"Let's see if this will work.
Poof!"

"Oh no!" Baby Shark says.

"My sand castle is shrinking."

"It's OK," Grandma Shark says.
"I'll get it right this time."

Grandma Shark casts her spell
and the sand castle
grows bigger.

It's the biggest sand castle ever!
Even a broken wand
can't spoil the fun!

"Hooray!" Baby Shark says.
"I love my magical grandma!"